Oh me,
oh my,
a
PIE!

First published 2018 by Nosy Crow Ltd
The Crow's Nest, 14 Baden Place,
Crosby Row, London SE1 1YW
www.nosycrow.com

ISBN 978 1 78800 102 1 (HB)
ISBN 978 1 78800 103 8 (PB)

Nosy Crow and associated logos are trademarks
and/or registered trademarks of Nosy Crow Ltd.

Text and illustrations © Jan Fearnley 2018

The right of Jan Fearnley to be identified as the author
and illustrator of this work has been asserted.

A CIP catalogue record for this book is available
from the British Library.

Printed in China

Papers used by Nosy Crow are made
from wood grown in sustainable forests.

1 3 5 7 9 8 6 4 2 (HB)
1 3 5 7 9 8 6 4 2 (PB)

FOR The yummy Aiden, Rose and Mam

Oh me, oh my, a PIE!

cooked up by

Jan Fearnley

nosy crow

A nice old grandma baked a pie.
It smelled so good – oh me, oh my!

"Yum! Yum!"
said Grandma to herself . . .

. . . and left it cooling on the shelf.

But, dear oh dear, I have to say . . .

that pie was **stolen** clean away.

A fox came by
with greedy eyes.
"Yum! Yum! A pie!
What a surprise!

I'll sneak it back into my lair
and, quickly, I'll devour it there.

Look what I've got. I've **pinched** a pie!
I'll eat the lot – oh me, oh my!"

So Fox ran off, his red tail flowing,
but didn't look where he was going . . .

The pie flew up into the sky . . .

then tumbled down –
oh me, oh my!

It landed near
a hungry mouse.

"I'll take this pie
back to my house.
Oh me, oh my –

this pie smells yummy!
I want this pie
inside my tummy!

Look what I've got. I've **found** a pie!
I'll eat the lot – oh me, oh my!"
Off scurried Mouse, on tiny feet.
He rolled the pie right down the street.

But then . . .

"Meow!

It's my pie now!"
A greedy cat stood in the street.
"I think I've found myself a treat.

Look what I've got —
a mouse, a pie!
I'll have you both —
oh me, oh my!"

So, off ran Cat, without delay.

But **somebody** stood in his way.
And . . .

WOOF! WOOF!

You've had enough!
This pie is mine.
Don't like it? **Tough!**

Yum! Yum!" said Dog.
"I think you'll see
this tasty pie
is meant for me.

Look what I've got.

I've grabbed a pie!
I'll wolf the lot – oh me, oh my!"

And off Dog scampered, with the pie,
while someone circled in the sky.

Plucked from Dog's paws . . .
off the pie flew.

"Too-wit! Too-woo! I want it too!"
said Little Owl, with flapping wings.
"Fresh pie is just my favourite thing!
Look what I've got. I've snatched the pie!
I'll scoff the lot – oh me, oh my!"

TO THE TOWN

So, off flew Owl,
back to her nest.
The pie was big.
She did her best.

But . . .

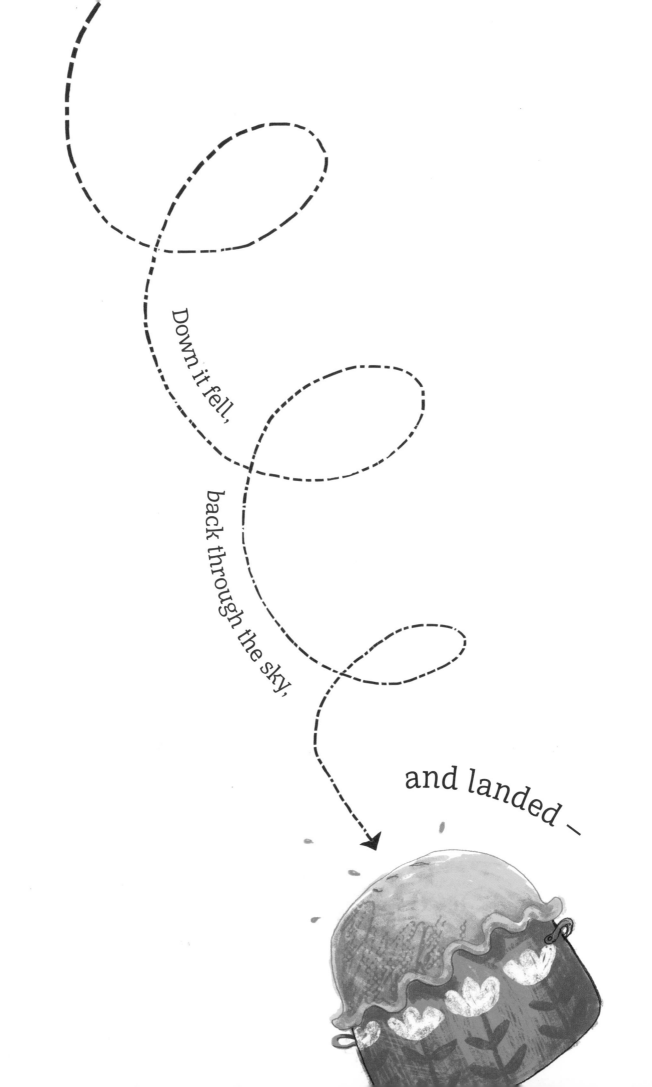

Down it fell,

back through the sky,

and landed –

THUD!

– oh me, oh my! –
back at the house,
as you can see . . .

DON'T Feed the Bears

and just in time for Grandma's tea.

Those greedy creatures all made haste
and soon arrived at Grandma's place.
But Grandma took the pie inside
and everybody wailed and cried.

"Oh, Grandma, please don't be a tease!
Give us some pie. Oh, Grandma, please!"
"Goodness!" said Grandma. "What a din!
I think you'd better all come in!

Now, you sit there. And you sit there.
You **can** have pie if you can share."

But . . .

. . . dear oh dear, I have to say,
those greedy creatures spoiled her day.

That silly lot, they wouldn't learn
that sometimes we must wait our turn.
They bickered and began to shout . . .

DON'T
Feed
the
Bears

till Grandma Bear said,
"OUT! OUT! OUT!"

She took her pie down from the shelf.
And Grandma . . .

ate it
ALL
HERSELF!